Enjoy All the S.O.S. Adventures!

HARPER **Chapters**

S.O.S.

SOCIETY OF SUBSTITUTES

Super Fun World

By Alan Katz

Illustrated by Alex Lopez

HARPER

An Imprint of HarperCollins*Publishers*

To Simone, Andrew, Nathan, and David . . . superheroes all.

—Alan Katz

S.O.S.: Society of Substitutes #4: Super Fun World

Library of Congress Control Number: 2021939632
ISBN 978-0-06-290943-5 — ISBN 978-0-06-290944-2 (pbk.)

Typography by Corina Lupp
21 22 23 24 25   PC/LSCC   10 9 8 7 6 5 4 3 2 1

First Edition

TABLE OF CONTENTS

CHAPTER 1

Coming Home

IT'S FINALLY TIME TO
YELL AND SHRIEK,
'CAUSE THERE'S NO SCHOOL
FOR ONE WHOLE WEEK!

It should have been a joyous bus ride home. After all, it was a Friday afternoon before the start of vacation week. Mrs. Baltman's sign had told her students she wouldn't see them again for nine days.

But as the bus creaked along Stagecoach Circle, Milton Worthy thought about something that Mrs. Baltman had said. It was nine words she'd said only to him, and he was pretty sure those words would ruin his entire vacation:

"Milton, please take Noah home for the vacation week."

When the bus stopped, Milton grabbed his stuff and clumsily got off in front of his house. His mother opened the front door and smiled widely, ready to share a vacation-starting hug with her son.

But when she saw what he was carrying, she too had nine words to say:

"Why in the world did you bring Noah home?"

"I didn't want to, Mom," Milton told her. "But Mrs. Baltman said that *someone* had to watch our class ferret over the break."

"I suppose that's true," Mrs. Worthy said. "But why not your friend Morgan? Or Max? Or David? Or *anyone else*?"

"I suggested them, believe me," Milton responded. "But Mrs. Baltman knows that Noah has a habit of escaping. She also knows that if he tries to take over the world again, only our family can stop him."

"I suppose that's also true," Mrs. Worthy told her son. "While Max's father is an apartment building *super,* and Morgan's sells *hero* sandwiches, I'm the only *superhero* in the neighborhood."

Milton agreed. Then he asked the question that had been rolling around in his brain since he got the Noah news:

"Does this mean our first-time-ever family vacation to Super Fun World is canceled?" Milton asked. "Please say no, please say no, please say no."

"No," his mother said.

"No, you're not saying *no*?" he asked. "Or no, it's not canceled?"

"No, it's not canceled," Mrs. Worthy assured him. "We've all been looking forward to it for months. We already paid for the theme park tickets and hotel. We'll just take Noah with us—we can't let two pounds of fur keep us from eleven tons of fun."

Milton jumped up and down and gave his mother the vacation-starting hug she'd wanted earlier.

Noah, however, wasn't nearly as gleeful. And oddly enough, he

expressed his displeasure in exactly nine words:

"Blotz-chitter-errp-chitter-blotz-mucky-freg-freg-nepp!"

Mrs. Worthy was wearing her official Society of Substitutes ferret decoder ring, so she knew that Noah said . . .

What do you think Noah's got planned?

1 ☐ ☐ ☐ ☐ ☐ ☐ ☐ ☐ ☐ ☐ ☐

On the Road

"You think you're taking me to Super Fun World. But when I get there, it won't be 'super' for you. It won't be 'fun' either. And as for the 'world' part—yes, there will still be a world. And it will be mine, all mine."

Clearly, Noah had the amazing ability to say a lot in only nine words.

The next morning, the Worthy family left bright and early. Mr. and Mrs. Worthy sat in the front seat, and Milton and his sister, Amy, were buckled into the back seat. Noah was tucked safely in the SUV's rear cargo area. His steel-reinforced Megabolt-5000 cage was locked tightly shut.

As soon as the family car left the driveway, Milton asked his mom for the Super Fun World map. He wanted to study it so that he could plot out each day's activities. But Milton's mother told him that, unfortunately, she had tucked the map into the outer pocket of her backpack. It was in the cargo area, alongside the other suitcases . . . and Noah's cage.

Milton knew he couldn't reach the map while buckled into his seat. He just shrugged and told his mom that he'd look at it when they got to the hotel.

Hearing where the map was made the only ferret in the car quite joyful. Noah slyly managed to sneak his paw through the bars of his mega-locked cage. And then he skillfully grabbed the Super Fun World map and quietly slid it into his cage.

As Mr. Worthy steered the car onto the highway, Milton's father yelled, "Here we go!"

Then he invited everyone to sing the song from the Super Fun World commercial:

Not just fun, but super fun
Super fun for everyone!
Rides and games and shows and food
To put you in a super fun mood!
Moms and dads and boys and girls
Head on down to Super Fun World!

Milton adored that song. He'd sung himself

to sleep with it for weeks (though he did wonder why they rhymed *girls* with *World*). No matter; he was sure their rides and games and shows and food would be even better than their jingle.

Noah, of course, didn't sing along. But he did enjoy the noise the singing made—it covered up the map-unfolding sound in his cage.

Noah spent the rest of the trip studying the map. Busily licking and scratching to mark the areas that would be important to his quest for world domination, he chittered happily.

He nibbled a few num-nums, then chased around his cage with excitement.

Meanwhile, Milton and Amy played tic-tac. (The little girl didn't have the patience to go all the way to toe. Instead, she yelled, "I win!" each time she got two in a row. And sometimes one in a row.)

Something like that usually would've driven Milton crazy. But somehow, knowing that the family was on its way to Super Fun World allowed him to ignore her silliness.

"This is going to be the greatest trip ever. Ever. E-V-E-R," Milton said aloud, momentarily forgetting that Noah was with them.

"Bleg. Bleg. B-L-E-G," Noah said aloud, not caring that the Worthy family was with him.

Checking In

As Mr. Worthy parked in front of the hotel, Milton yelled, "We're heeeeeere!" Three bellhops dressed like polar bears swooped in and started removing everything from the SUV's cargo area. Before the four Worthy family members could exit the car, their bags (and Noah's cage!) were whisked away to the hotel.

The Worthys stepped up to the check-in desk. A super friendly desk clerk welcomed them by name, smiled an extra wide Super Fun World

Hotel smile, then gave them some bad news . . .

"You can't check into your room for two more hours."

"What?" Milton exclaimed.

"I said, you can't check into your room for two more hours," said Melody the clerk. "But you're all welcome to have a super fun time in our super fun lobby."

"What is there to do in the lobby?" Milton asked her.

"There's a super fun couch, super fun chairs, super fun footstools, and some super fun magazines," Melody said. "Go enjoy yourselves, and come back for the keys to your super fun room at three."

"Couch?" Mrs. Worthy asked.

"Chairs?" her daughter asked.

"Footstools and magazines?" Mr. Worthy asked.

"We want real super fun, and we'll only find that inside the gates of Super Fun World!"

Milton said. "Let's go!"

"Now?" Mr. Worthy asked his son.

"Why not?" he replied. "We have prepaid tickets. We can go to the park, then come back tonight. The room will still be here, right?"

"You're right," Mrs. Worthy said. "And so will the couch, the chairs, the footstools, and the magazines."

"So . . . let's go to Super Fun World!" all four Worthys shouted.

19

Mr. Worthy asked Melody to have the polar bear bellhops put their things in storage. He told her they'd be back to check in later that evening.

Melody agreed, and the family watched as their bags—and Noah's cage—were carried to the storage area. Milton gave Noah a *see ya later* wave as Ira the polar bear bellhop carefully placed Noah's cage on a shelf.

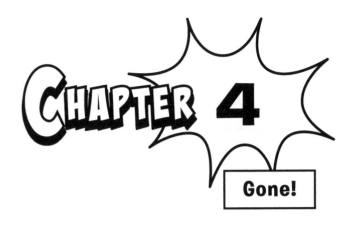

CHAPTER 4

Gone!

But as Ira turned to leave, Noah started whining and crying. His blubbering made Ira blubber too. And if there's anything sadder than a blubbering ferret, it's a grown man who's blubbering while wearing a polar bear costume.

Ira couldn't stand to see the ferret so upset. He asked Noah if he was hungry.

Noah shook his head *no*.

Ira asked Noah if he was thirsty.

Noah shook his head *no*.

Ira asked Noah if his tummy hurt.

Noah shook his head *no*.

Ira asked Noah if he needed a good stretch.

Noah nodded his head *yes*.

"Gee, I'd be glad to let you out for a minute, buddy," Ira told the ferret through his tears. "But this cage is the Megabolt-5000. There's practically no way to open it without detailed instructions."

Noah spun around several times with glee,

then tipped the cage's hangtag toward Ira's face. On the hangtag was the Beacher Elementary School address. And behind that, Ira found . . .

. . . detailed instructions.

So Ira dried his own tears and did the one thing he shouldn't have done. He reached for the Megabolt-5000 cage and followed the detailed instructions. In a flash, Noah was in his arms.

"There, little guy," Ira said. "Give yourself a good little stretch, then we'll put you back inside the Megabolt-5000."

Noah hugged Ira in appreciation. For about .0337 of a second. Then Noah giggled a sinister giggle and leapt out of the polar bear bellhop's grasp. He zipped off, climbing over suitcases, shelves, desks, and pretty much everything in his way.

"Um, er, wait, ah, I mean, come back, please," Ira said as he started to blubber again. "Why, that ferret tricked me!" he told himself. "But I'll fix this mess, or my name isn't . . ."

He looked down at his name badge.

"Ira."

Ira put on his official polar bear thinking cap. He thought about reporting the runaway ferret to the head of the polar bear bellhops.

He considered running around the hotel in search of the critter.

He pondered going to the local pet store and buying a replacement ferret.

"A ferret is a ferret is a ferret," Ira told himself. "The family will never know."

But then Ira realized that it wasn't the most honest approach to fixing the problem. So he thought some more, and remembered something his grandfather had once told him:

"Little Bo-Peep has lost her sheep and doesn't know where to find them. Leave them alone, and they'll come home, wagging their tails behind them."

Ira knew that ferrets weren't exactly the same as sheep. But he had confidence in his grandfather's words. So he put the whole situation out of his mind and went to have a snack.

Meanwhile, at Super Fun World, the Worthy family was having . . .

Way to go! You've read 1,792 words. Congratulations!

1 2 3 4 ☐ ☐ ☐ ☐ ☐ ☐ ☐ ☐

CHAPTER 5

Super Fun!

What else? Super fun!

Milton and his mom had already been on seven rides, including the Fuming Flume of Doom and the Roaster Toaster Coaster. (Mom almost lost her backpack—and her lunch—on that coaster.)

Amy and Dad had taken five trips through Mr. Chicken's Hilarious Henhouse. And each time they exited, Mr. Chicken wished them the best of cluck.

It wasn't that Mr. Worthy was afraid of thrill rides. It was just that he suffered from a sore back, so he volunteered to experience the tamer attractions with Amy.

Plus, he was a *little* afraid of thrill rides.

Mr. and Mrs. Worthy agreed that the family members would meet at the entrance to Princess Monica's Castle at 7 p.m.

"I think we've got time for a couple more rides,

Milton. What's your pleasure?" his mom asked.
She was secretly hoping for a long ride on a park
bench—to relax. But she knew that Milton was
determined to take on every heart-stopping ride
in the park.

Milton looked at his map, which was a little
scrunched because he'd squeezed it so tightly
while riding Mission to Boingo.

"Double Dip Dilemma looks good," he answered. "Unless you'd rather try the Stomach Rumble Grumbler."

"They both sound delightful," Mrs. Worthy said through gritted teeth as she tightened the buckles on her backpack.

Milton saw that the line was shorter on the Grumbler, so that was where they went.

A few moments later, they were fastening their seatbelts and lowering their shoulder harnesses.

"Please remember that you will be upside down during most of this ride," the attendant announced. "Keep your hands inside the car at all times. Please tuck your phones securely in your pockets. And if you have fake teeth, be sure to keep them in your mouth. Last week, someone's dentures went flying, and they ended up biting a woman down on the ground."

The ride started. The car that held Mrs. Worthy and Milton went up . . . up . . . up the track. Then it went down . . . up . . . down . . . and upside down. It stayed upside down for a long time, which didn't make Mrs. Worthy feel so great.

Milton, on the other hand, repeatedly squealed with glee. He even yelled, "Now *this* is super fun!"

Then . . . without the ride having moved at all, Milton began to shriek. It wasn't an *I'm loving*

this shriek. Rather, it was a *something's wrong, very wrong, very, very wrong* kind of sound. He uttered a phrase that combined "Oh no!" with "I don't believe it!" and "It can't be!"

Mrs. Worthy thought that Milton was terrified of the ride. But it wasn't the Stomach Rumble Grumbler that made him howl with fear.

It was . . .

CHAPTER 6

Taking Action

Noah!

While upside down on the ride, Milton spotted the evildoing, sinister ferret running through the park.

Just as soon as the Stomach Rumble Grumbler stopped, Milton told his mom what he had seen. She tried to convince him that he had probably just spotted one of the park's costumed characters. But Milton said he *knew* that it was Noah, ready to cause trouble. Big trouble.

Mrs. Worthy led Milton into a quiet area just behind the Franks-A-Lot hot dog stand. She told her son that there was no time to lose.

"Though I'm usually a superhero substitute teacher, I think I'd better go into evil-fighting mode at once," she told him. "With so many people, and so many rides, there's so much chaos a nasty ferret could cause!"

"I understand, Mom" Milton said.

"There's just one problem," Mrs. Worthy moaned. "If I turn into a superhero right in public, everyone will know my secret identity!"

"Mom, there are costumed superhero characters all over this park. No one will know you're a *real* one!" Milton pointed out.

Mrs. Worthy thought that was an excellent point.

Milton watched breathlessly as his mom reached into her backpack and put on her Society of Substitutes transmitter helmet. She pressed the communicator button and called Chief Chiefman at headquarters. Surely the chief would know what was up with Noah—and what to do about it.

"I see. Yes. I see. I understand. Oh my. Wow. Yes, I see," Mrs. Worthy said into the communicator. "Goodbye, Chief. And thank you."

As Mrs. Worthy disconnected the call and put her helmet back in her backpack, Milton asked his mom if it was a serious problem.

Mrs. Worthy told him yes, quite serious. But this time, Noah wasn't actually seeking to rule the world. Or the country. He wasn't trying to take over the town, or even Super Fun World. He had one very specific target in mind, and he had a plan to make his dream a reality.

Noah was solely interested in getting rid of . . .

Rose Worthy!

"I was right to worry about protecting my superhero identity, Milton," Mrs. Worthy said. "Noah wants to expose me as a member of the Society of Substitutes."

"Would that be bad, Mom?" Milton wanted to know.

"Bad? It would be *terrible!*" Mrs. Worthy replied.

She said that revealing her true superhero identity would be a big first step toward Noah's goal of total world domination.

Milton asked why, and she said there was no time to explain at the moment. First, they had to stop Noah.

"According to Chief Chiefman, Noah has snapped a photo of me in my full superhero gear.

He plans to put that photo on the big video screen during Super Fun World's fireworks show tonight."

"That's great!" Milton beamed.

"What's great about it?" his mother wanted to know.

"It means we can stay for the fireworks!" Milton cheered.

"Never mind that," Mrs. Worthy said. "We've got to catch that furry fiend and stop him before he discloses that I'm a real-life superhero!"

"Gotcha, Mom," Milton said. "Look, it's six fifty-five. We are supposed to meet Dad and Sis in five minutes."

"You're right, Milton. I'll text Dad and tell him to take Amy to Mr. Chicken's Hilarious Henhouse. We can meet them later."

Mrs. Worthy quickly texted her husband the message. He immediately wrote back:

Mrs. Worthy wrote back:

"Poor Dad," Mrs. Worthy said, adding, "but that ratty rascal has to be stopped!"

"Dad isn't a ratty rascal," Milton said.

"I meant Noah, silly boy," his mother told him. "If Dad watches Amy, I can go after Noah."

"You mean *we* can," Milton said.

"Yes, I suppose *we* can," Mrs. Worthy said.

Mrs. Worthy took all her superhero gear out of her backpack. She tucked her Official S.O.S. Num-Num Launcher into her jeans. She also placed her Fabulous Ferret Finder hair scrunchie on her head. The F.F.F. was guaranteed to ferret out any ferret.

"Hey, Mom, do *I* get any gear?" Milton asked.

"I'm sorry, but these evil-fighting tools are for superheroes only," Mrs. Worthy said. "They're not for superheroes' sons."

47

"Mom, look at it this way," Milton told her. "If you give me a gadget and I help save the world, that's a good thing. The chief couldn't possibly be mad, right?"

Mrs. Worthy considered what Milton was saying.

Milton continued. "And if I *don't* have anything, and the world explodes or something, the

chief *would* be mad. Well, he'd be exploded. But right before exploding, he'd be mad. Right?"

Mrs. Worthy couldn't argue with Milton's logic. So she reached into her backpack and gave her son . . .

What kind of superhero gadget would you want to have to stop Noah?

1 2 3 4 5 6 7 □ □ □ □ □ □

CHAPTER 8

Find That Ferret

"A harmonica, Mom?" Milton asked. "What am I going to do, play 'Hot Cross Buns' and *bore* Noah out of hiding?"

"No, Milton," his mother answered. "That may *look* like a regular harmonica, but in fact, it's a superpowered megaphone. Speak loudly into that and people will hear you all over the park."

"A har-megaphone? Coooool!" Milton said.

"But do not, do not, do not use it unless absolutely necessary!" his mother warned. "Believe me, it's loud."

"Okay, Mom. Thanks!" Milton said as he tucked the device into his pocket.

Mrs. Worthy flipped the switch on her Fabulous Ferret Finder hair scrunchie, and it started beeping. She took a step forward and it beeped louder. Another step, louder. Then she turned to the right. Softer. She turned around to walk in the other direction. Louder.

She and Milton continued on that path until the loud beeping was replaced by a *ding-ding-ding*. Mrs. Worthy looked up and noticed that the scrunchie had led her to the business headquarters of Super Fun World.

"My Fabulous Ferret Finder says Noah is inside this building," Mrs. Worthy said. "But why?"

"Gee, Mom," Milton replied. "Maybe that's where they keep the video equipment that Noah needs to use to put your picture on the big screen. He might be uploading it right now."

Mrs. Worthy thought about that. Then she said, "Milton, give me the har-megaphone."

Milton didn't understand why she wanted it.

He thought perhaps he was in trouble for something. But that wasn't the case at all.

Instead, Mrs. Worthy put the har-megaphone far in front of her mouth and said softly, "Noah, come out here. We've got you cornered."

But when Noah *did* come outside, he just blew them a sinister kiss and then scampered off.

"Let's get him!" Milton shouted.

But Mrs. Worthy didn't chase after the ferret. Instead, she led Milton into the building and found the video control center.

Milton was right. Noah had uploaded the photo, and it was set to display on the big screen at 8 p.m. . . . right before the fireworks!

"I'm afraid the photo is already programmed in, and it's set to be shown at eight," Mrs. Worthy said. "I'm doomed."

"Doomed, Mom?" Milton asked. "I don't think so! Follow me!"

CHAPTER 9

What's a P.E.C.K.?

Milton escorted his mother out of the building.

"Where are we going?" she wanted to know.

"There's only one thing better than having a Fabulous Ferret Finder," Milton told her.

"And that's having a genius son. I am one hundred percent sure I know where Noah is."

With his mom following, Milton led the way to the main stage, just outside Princess Monica's Castle.

"This is where they're going to show my picture and ruin my superhero life," Mrs. Worthy said. She pointed to the giant video screen above

the Super Fun World stage.

"Right, Mom," Milton agreed. "But . . . if Noah set that up, he's certainly going to want to watch it, right?'

"You're right, Milton. *There he is!*"

It was almost too easy. Noah was reclining on a park bench, staring up at the video screen with gleeful anticipation!

61

Milton and his mom tiptoed up behind Noah.

"Good thing I brought along my P.E.C.K.," Mrs. Worthy whispered.

"Yeah, definitely, it sure is," Milton whispered back, before adding, "What in the world is a P.E.C.K.?"

"My Portable Emergency Cage Keeper, of course," Mrs. Worthy responded. "You grab Noah, and I'll toss the self-opening P.E.C.K. onto him!"

"Okay," Milton whispered. "On the count of three?"

"No, two," his mother said. "At the Society of Substitutes, we know that time is of the essence. We always act on the count of two, since in a true emergency, there may not be time to count to three."

"I could have counted to twenty-six during that explanation, Mom," Milton pointed out. "But okay, let's do it on the count of two. One . . . two!"

Only three more chapters to go! How do you think this will end?

Backstage

Mrs. Worthy jumped into action. And before Noah knew what was happening, he was safe and secure in the P.E.C.K.

The ferret squirmed. He curled. He twisted. But it all did no good; he quickly realized that he was trapped!

Noah was furious, but he knew that Mrs. Worthy couldn't do anything to stop her photo from being shown on the big video screen. He also knew that she knew that, and he knew that she knew that he knew that she knew that.

Mrs. Worthy had to find a way to stop her photo and superhero identity from being displayed on the video board. As she thought about what to do, Milton offered some suggestions.

Milton wasn't sure what he'd said, but he was glad his mother liked it.

Mrs. Worthy pointed to the stage right below the video screen. She told Milton to wait for his dad and sister, then bring them to meet her backstage. She kissed her son, then ran off with Noah in the P.E.C.K.

A few minutes later, Milton's father and Amy came by. Having visited Mr. Chicken's Hilarious Henhouse 117 times, Mr. Worthy now walked like a chicken. In fact, it was more like a barnyard dance than a walk. What's more, he struggled to speak, and clucked out his words instead. He told Milton:

CLUCKETY-CLUCK, CLUCKETY-COO, MILTON, IT'S GOOD TO COCK-A-DOODLE-DOO SEE YOU!

Milton laughed. He laughed again when Amy clucked out the same message.

Milton then led his poultry parent and baby chick sister to the backstage area.

With Noah safely tucked away in the P.E.C.K., Mrs. Worthy quickly described her plan to her husband and daughter. She said:

"Don't ask questions, just please do what I ask. I need to distract the large crowd. I'm

thinking we could perform the song we did for the family talent show at Milton's school. It was a big hit! Does everyone remember the lyrics?"

"Cluck," said Mr. Worthy.

"Cluck, cluck," said his daughter.

"Oh no!" said Mrs. Worthy.

How do you think Milton and his mom will save the day?

CHAPTER 11

Poultry in Motion

"Mom," Milton explained, "I think Dad and Sis spent a little too much time in Mr. Chicken's Hilarious Henhouse."

"Cluck 117 times cluck-cluck," Mr. Worthy confirmed.

"I don't think they're going to be able to perform our big talent show song," Mrs. Worthy observed sadly.

"You might be right," Milton said. "But, Mom . . . what could be more distracting

than a man and his daughter clucking around
onstage?"

"Milton, you are a triple genius," Mrs. Worthy said. Then she noticed that it was 7:58 p.m.; just two minutes before her superhero picture was going to be shown onscreen.

She grabbed the har-megaphone and said, "Ladies and gentlemen, please welcome tonight's mega-talented special guests, The Chicken Family!"

Mr. Worthy led the family onstage. He was walking like a chicken and clucking. Amy was doing the same. So were Milton and his mom.

They danced and clucked. They clucked and danced. It was a crazy sight. A crazy, crazy, crazy sight. And it didn't merely distract the crowd from looking at the screen—it sent them scurrying toward the Super Fun World exits.

75

When the clock struck 8 p.m., Mrs. Worthy's superhero photo was indeed shown on the screen. But the good news was . . . there was absolutely no one there to see it.

Problem solved. So Mrs. Worthy took Noah, her son, and their two chicken-y relatives back to the Super Fun World Hotel.

Once they arrived, Mrs. Worthy asked Frank the polar bear bellhop to collect their bags from the storage room. In a flash, he brought their suitcases and Noah's empty cage into the lobby.

As her husband and daughter clucked and pecked water from the fountain, Mrs. Worthy carefully put Noah back into his cage. Then she folded up the P.E.C.K. and put it away, hoping she wouldn't need to use it again.

Just then, Ira walked by. He looked at Noah in his cage and screamed out, "Just as Grandpa said! Leave them alone and they'll come home, wagging their tails behind them!"

No one knew what Ira meant. Besides, everyone was trying to figure out what to do about the two chicken-people who were now bathing in the fountain.

CHAPTER 12

And Finally . . .

Compared to that first day, the rest of the vacation was quiet. Mr. Worthy and his daughter woke up just fine the next morning. No chicken-y behavior at all, though for some strange reason, Mr. Worthy suddenly enjoyed licking his fingers.

With Noah securely locked in the Megabolt-5000, the Worthy family spent a super fun week going on rides (*not* the Henhouse). They played games. They saw fireworks and shows. And they all had a blast.

The vacation week soon ended, as all vacation weeks do. And on the ride home, with his dad and Amy sound asleep in the back seat, Milton was curious about something.

"Hey, Mom," the boy asked. "How come you really wanted to keep your superhero identity a secret?"

"Good question, Milton," she said. "If Noah had exposed me as a real superhero, it could have prevented me from performing my future duties. Stopping bad guys—or bad ferrets, in this case—in their tracks requires the element of surprise. Being known as a superhero would take away any chance of that surprise. Get it?"

"I think so, Mom," Milton told his mom.

"Remember, son," Mrs. Worthy added, "to the world, I am a regular substitute teacher. It's only when needed that I become a superhero."

"Got it, Mom."

"I can never allow anything to reveal that I am a superhero, son," Mrs. Worthy said. "Nothing at all."

Then she checked that her husband and Amy were still sleeping and put the SUV into SuperTurboDrive. It soared high above the highway and the trees and landed in the Worthys' driveway within minutes.

Back at Beacher Elementary School on Monday, there was a funny sign from Mrs. Baltman put up in Room 311B. It read:

YOU JUST WENT A WEEK
WITHOUT EDUKATION,
HOPE YOU HAD A NICE
VAKASHUN

Milton thought that sign was hilarious. But the ferret he was carrying didn't laugh one bit.

Milton told all his friends what a great time he had at Super Fun World. He made it sound like the best week ever.

The more Milton raved about Super Fun World, the madder Noah got. After all, Noah knew the truth. He knew he had escaped. He knew that Mr. Worthy and Amy had spent hours acting like chickens. And he knew he'd had a foolproof plan to expose Mrs. Worthy as a superhero (well, an *almost* foolproof plan).

Noah was too angry to chitter or chirp. Instead, he just sputtered some sinister sounds to tell the world that, without question . . . this wasn't over. This wasn't over at all.

The end.

(For now.)

CONGRATULATIONS!

You've read **12** chapters,

87 pages,

and **5,013** words!

All your super-sleuthing paid off!

SUPER AWESOME GAMES

Think

Milton loves going on rides. If there are thirty-five rides at Super Fun World and Milton and his family are there for a whole week, how many rides does Milton have to go on every day in order to ride them all?

Feel

In the story, the family has to go onstage to foil Noah's plans. Can you think of a time that you had to talk in front of a big group of people? Write about what happened and how you felt after.

Act

Milton's dad and his sister, Amy, don't like scary rides. What's the biggest, scariest amusement park ride you've ever gone on? Draw a picture of the ride.

Alan Katz has written more than forty books, including *Take Me Out of the Bathtub and Other Silly Dilly Songs*, *The Day the Mustache Took Over*, *OOPS!*, and *Really Stupid Stories for Really Smart Kids*. He has received many awards for his writing, and he loves visiting schools across the country.

Alex Lopez was born in Sabadell, a city in Spain near Barcelona. Alex has always loved to draw. His work has been featured in many books in many countries, but nowadays, he focuses mostly on illustrating books for young readers and teens.